Alexander Thom und Co.

Return of judicial rents fixed by Sub-Commissions and Civil Bill Courts

Courts

Notified to Irish Land Commission, October 1885

Alexander Thom und Co.

Return of judicial rents fixed by Sub-Commissions and Civil Bill Courts
Notified to Irish Land Commission, October 1885

ISBN/EAN: 9783742805904

Manufactured in Europe, USA, Canada, Australia, Japa

Cover: Foto ©Andreas Hilbeck / pixelio.de

Manufactured and distributed by brebook publishing software
(www.brebook.com)

Alexander Thom und Co.

Return of judicial rents fixed by Sub-Commissions and Civil Bill Courts

Irish Land Commission.

The Land Law (Ireland) Act, 1881, 44 & 45 Victoria, ch. 49

RETURN

ACCORDING TO PROVINCES AND COUNTIES

of

JUDICIAL RENTS

FIXED BY

SUB-COMMISSIONS

AND

CIVIL BILL COURTS,

AS NOTIFIED TO THE IRISH LAND COMMISSION DURING THE MONTH OF

OCTOBER, 1885,

SPECIFYING DATES AND AMOUNTS RESPECTIVELY OF THE LAST INCREASES OF RENT WHERE ASCERTAINED;

ALSO

RENTS FIXED UPON THE REPORTS OF VALUERS APPOINTED BY THE IRISH LAND COMMISSION ON THE JOINT APPLICATIONS OF LANDLORDS AND TENANTS.

Presented to both Houses of Parliament by Command of Her Majesty.

DUBLIN:
PRINTED BY ALEX. THOM & CO. (LIMITED), 87, 88, & 89, ABBEY-STREET,
THE QUEEN'S PRINTING OFFICE.

To be purchased, either directly or through any Bookseller, from any of the following Agents, viz :
Messrs. HANSARD, 13, Great Queen-street, W.C., and 32, Abingdon-street, Westminster;
Messrs. EYRE and SPOTTISWOODE, East Harding-street, Fleet-street, and Sale Office, House of Lords;
Messrs. ADAM and CHARLES BLACK, of Edinburgh:
Messrs. ALEX. THOM and Co. (Limited), or Messrs. HODGES, FIGGIS, and Co., of Dublin.

1886.

INDEX.

SUMMARY.

Showing, according to Provinces and Counties, the Number of Cases in which Judicial Rents have been Fixed by Sub-Commissions during the Month of October, 1885; and also the Acreages, Tenement Valuations, Former Rents, and Judicial Rents of the Holdings.

Provinces and Counties	Number of Cases in which Judicial Rents have been Fixed	Acreage	Tenement Valuation	Former Rent	Judicial Rent
		Statute Acres	£ s. d.	£ s. d.	£ s. d.
ULSTER—					
Armagh,	19	330 3 16	270 5 0	290 3 10	205 16 0
Cavan,	26	571 0 1	301 11 0	407 11 10	236 16 0
Fermanagh,	11	249 2 28	85 0 0	160 1 7	117 12 8
Monaghan,	20	272 2 16	192 10 0	813 3 0½	169 13 2
Tyrone,	76	1,530 3 7	819 17 2	851 0 0	744 16 8
Total,	145	3,048 3 21	1,696 3 3	2,004 3 3½	1,567 15 8
LEINSTER—					
Kilkenny,	15	749 0 3	657 5 0	636 8 8	538 1 6
King's County,	16	669 1 29	347 1 0	371 1 4	330 6 8
Longford,	4	263 2 37	347 5 0	277 1 8	255 10 8
Queen's County,	20	894 1 16	516 12 0	829 10 1	611 10 0
Wexford,	16	716 2 37	423 10 0	645 7 9	435 18 8
Total,	63	3,287 1 2	2,271 13 8	2,816 7 5	2,153 17 6
CONNAUGHT—					
Galway,	20	296 0 25	90 10 6	110 10 0	94 17 8
Leitrim,	33	946 2 27½	224 3 8	328 15 0	248 13 8
Mayo,	19	291 0 19	76 9 0	106 11 0	83 1 8
Roscommon,	17	336 2 11	184 15 0	379 17 4	166 13 4
Sligo,	18	1,315 5 33½	173 10 0	625 19 11	442 17 8
Total,	127	3,270 2 5½	1,111 7 0	1,121 11 3	1,840 2 0
MUNSTER—					
Clare,	71	2,371 1 0	1,178 15 0	1,696 8 9	1,398 17 8
Cork,	1	13 0 28	9 10 0	13 17 0	11 10 0
Kerry,	71	3,108 3 15	1,621 15 0	2,859 2 3	2,131 3 8
Tipperary,	16	634 3 12	703 5 0	530 0 1	173 11 7
Waterford,	7	191 2 15	117 10 0	213 1 6	164 10 0
Total,	168	7,750 0 6	3,640 11 0	5,454 16 6	6,375 1 10

IRELAND.

ULSTER,	145	3,048 3 24	1,696 3 2	2,004 3 8½	1,562 15 6
LEINSTER,	63	3,297 1 2	3,271 18 0	2,815 7 8	2,158 17
CONNAUGHT,	127	3,270 2 5½	1,114 7 0	1,421 14 8	1,840 2 0
MUNSTER,	168	7,750 0 8	3,663 11 0	5,654 16 6	4,375 1 10
TOTAL,	523	17,466 2 30¼	8,743 14 2	11,896 1 5½	9,931 16 10

Note.—For Cork Hill Court on terms, see page 11

o

D

Names of Annual Commissioners by whom Cases were decided.	No.	Name of Tenant.	Name of Landlord.	Townland.
Assistant Commissioners—				
R. R. Kane (Legal), B. Garland, E. R. Bayly.	5113	John Cornill, ...	Mrs. Esther McCombs, ...	Drumcrumugh, ...
	5114	William Irwin and anor., Admors. of D. W. Irwin.	Rev. F. C. Hardy and anor.,	Derrymacfall, ...
	5115	John Malloy, ...	John H. Portell, ...	Ahisig, ...
	5116	Alexander Bryson, ...	Mrs Eleanor Madore, ...	Ballinahone, ...
	5117	John Redmond, ...	F. B Cope, ...	Derrylaughan, ...
	5118	Thomas Taylor, ...	Earl of Charlemont, ...	Gledymire, ...
	5119	Thomas McClure, ...	Louisa Donnelly and others,	Dromenhavill, ...
	5120	Paul Harron, ...	Lord Lurgan, ...	Tamnaghmore, West,
	5121	Thomas Mackan, ...	Thompson Woods, ...	Derryloy, ...
	5122	Michael McEvoy, ...	Miss Janette V. Bennett, ...	Fulhan, ...
	5123	Thomas Rooney, ...	Thomas A. Prentice and another, Trustees of H. L. Prentice.	Drumaunmond, ...
	5124	Ann Orr, ...	do. ...	do. ...
				Total, ...

	No.			
Assistant Commissioners—	2143	Robert Ferguson, ...	Samuel H. Maxwell, ...	Tullyboy, ...
R. R. Kane (Legal), B. Garland, M. R. Bayly.	2144	Do. ...	do. ...	Drumboe, ...
	2145	Thomas McMahon and anor., Reps. of Philip McMahon	Lord Charles De La P. Beresford.	Scrabby and anor.,
	2146	Patrick Donohoe, ...	do. ...	McCrystalstown,
	2147	James Taylor, ...	Genl F. Romer, ...	Cummeraghd, ...
	2148	Owen Mahon, ...	Lyndon Bolton, ...	Dottes, ...
	2149	John Brady, ...	J. W. Stanford, ...	Listernan, ...
	2150	Owen Dolan, ...	Earl Annesley, ...	Garvah, Upper,
	2151	Philip Mahon, ...	Rev. Richard Gumley, ...	Urater, ...
	2152	Hugh Reilly and another,	Hon. Clare Annesley, ...	Aghermore, ...
	2153	John J. Bennett, ...	do. ...	Marble, ...
	2154	Francis Dolan, ...	Lieut.-Col. H J. Jervis White,	Halfdevon, ...
	2155	Ellen McTeague, ...	do. ...	do. ...
	2156	Margaret Magennis, ...	do. ...	do. ...

ULSTER.

ARMAGH.

Amount of Holdery Statute	Poor Law Valuation	Former Rent	Judicial Rent	Observations	Value of Tenancy
A. R. P.	£ s. d.	£ s. d.	£ s. d.	£ s. d.	£ s. d.
37 1 10	36 15 0	31 14 0	24 3 0		
36 2 27	30 0 0	35 0 9	30 10 0		
19 0 5	54 10 0	43 15 0	42 0 0		
7 3 15	15 10 0	19 11 8	11 0 0		
5 3 30	8 0 0	8 5 0	5 10 0		
11 2 25	17 10 0	13 7 11	10 5 0		
25 1 0	17 15 0	16 10 9	12 10 0		
4 1 10	8 6 0	7 15 0	6 6 0		
3 0 10	5 5 0	8 5 0	6 0 0	Rent changed in 1857 from	8 0 0
13 1 39	10 0 0	11 7 6	8 0 0	1853	13 17 8
11 2 10	15 15 0	15 6 0	12 10 0		
39 3 23	51 0 0	60 7 8	16 0 0		
250 3 11	270 5 0	290 3 10	205 15 0		

CAVAN.

20 3 0	unascertained	21 0 0	18 10 0		
14 0 11	8 5 0	9 15 0	8 15 0		
15 1 38	10 10 0	13 0 0	13 0 0		
43 1 30	30 15 0	34 5 0	25 0 0		
26 2 5	18 0 0	21 10 0	17 15 0		
9 3 34	3 10 0	5 5 0	1 1 0		
5 0 15	4 13 0	4 15 0	5 15 0	Rent changed in 1864 from	1 4 0
17 0 16	3 5 0	5 0 0	3 5 0		
13 0 5	6 10 0	11 10 0	8 10 0		
37 1 35	16 10 0	14 5 8	12 10 0		
45 3 23	25 0 0	23 10 0	28 10 0		
27 1 4	16 15 0	18 4 8	13 5 0	By consent.	
28 1 0	13 5 0	16 5 0	13 5 0		
23 2 30	19 5 0	13 13 7	11 0 0	Rent changed in 1850 from	14 1 8

Names of Assistant Commissioners by whom Cases were decided.	No.	Name of Tenant.	Name of Landlord.	Townland.
Assistant Commissioners—				
B. B. Kane (Legal.)	7107	Jane Wallace, Admix. of Mathew Wallace.	Alfred Finlay and another,	Honeymore,
B. Garland.	8155	Hugh McGovern,	do.	Cloninly,
E. B. Bailie.	8129	Patrick McCauley,	do.	Eagle Hall,
	3160	Patrick Henry and another,	Francis Finlay and another,	do.
	7181	Patrick McGovern,	Alfred Finlay and another,	Clorbally,
	7169	Robert Ferguson,	Somerset H. Maxwell,	Tullyhoy,
	8162	Bridget Maguey, Admix. of James Maguey.	Colonel George M. Dobbin,	Mully, Lower,
	8164	John Curran,	Lord Charles Beresford,	Killymuckaham,
	8166	Eliza Maguire, Executrix of Thomas Maguire.	do.	Townagh,
	7166	Edward Rankin,	Michael O'Banks and others, Trustees of late Jas. O'Banks.	Owen Challan,
	8167	Eliza Maguire, Admix. of Thomas Maguire.	Lord Charles Beresford,	Sarabby,
	2168	John Maguire,	Earl Annesley,	Ligmalirk,
			Total,	

Names of Assistant Commissioners by whom Cases were decided.	No.	Name of Tenant.	Name of Landlord.	Townland.
Assistant Commissioners—				
B. B. Kane (Legal.)	7138	Andrew Irvine,	Captain M. Archdale,	Gortytown,
B. Garland.	7139	Irwin Elliott,	F. and L. Porter,	Mullaghleagh,
E. B. Bailie.	3510	Robert Reid,	J. G. V. Porter,	Lisnagh,
	7241	Alan Higgins,	Catherine B. Collum and ors.,	Inishkeen Island,
	8342	James Coyle,	William Archdale,	Drumherrin,
	2343	James McCaffrey,	John Wallace, and others,	Islandhill,
	3244	James Devitt,	John McBride,	Kilrooan,
	3315	Joseph Carr,	Lord Rathdonnell,	Knockmacahen,
	3346	George Bruce,	do.	do.
	3347	Patrick Maguire, jun.	Colonel J. G. Irvine,	Largy,
	7348	Patrick Maguire,	do.	do.
			Total,	

Extent of Holding Statute.	Poor Law Valuation.	Former Rent.	Judged Rent.	Observations.	Value of Tenancy.
a. r. p.	£ s. d.	£ s. d.	£ s. d.		£ s. d.
14 1 5	7 15 0	8 13 6	7 10 0		
15 0 0	7 10 0	9 5 0	6 0 0		
61 1 35	10 10 0	14 0 0	13 0 0		
8 3 14	3 0 0	6 0 0	4 0 0		
26 3 0	13 0 0	21 15 0	16 0 0		
17 2 0	unascertained.	14 0 0	13 0 0	Rent changed in 1870 from £5 1s. 3d. Provision has been made in this case as regards a labourer.	
34 0 30	6 10 0	12 16 4	8 10 0	Provision has been made in this case as regards a labourer.	
85 3 33	43 0 0	40 5 0	31 0 0	do.	
44 1 34	16 3 0	23 0 0	19 0 0	do.	
5 1 13	2 6 0	8 15 0	7 10 0	Rent changed in 1847 from . . . 5 9 11	
14 1 34	10 0 0	6 6 0	5 5 0		
171 1 0	11 10 0	18 0 0	11 0 0	By consent.	
873 0 1	301 11 0	507 14 10	394 19 0		

FERMANAGH.

16 0 16	13 10 0	13 0 0	11 5 0		
43 0 0	unascertained.	27 15 6	24 5 0		
12 3 14	7 10 0	7 10 3	7 10 3		
33 0 30	11 15 0	20 0 0	16 0 0	Rent changed in 1846 from . . . 18 16 0 1863 8 9 6	
7 0 0	unascertained.	6 0 0	4 0 0		
22 0 15	11 5 0	14 3 0	8 15 0		
13 0 10	10 0 0	9 1 3	8 10 0		
20 1 0	14 15 0	15 6 8	13 15 0		
31 0 30	15 5 0	13 10 0	11 15 0		
45 0 34	unascertained.	9 11 4	11 10 0		
36 0 0	do.	2 18 2	10 15 0		
342 3 23	83 0 0	140 1 7	137 19 9		

No.			
2542	Robert Graham, Exor. of Elizabeth Graham,	Miss Henrietta Westenra a lunatic by H. O Lewis, her Committee.	Mullaback,
2543	Margaret Mulligan,	do.	Stramackilroy,
2544	Do.,	do.	Stramboyne,
2545	George Haldcroft,	do.	Derrybrughass,
2546	John Smith,	do.	Bessmygragh,
2547	Patrick Herbert,	Dacre Hamilton,	Killyhunkicorn,
2548	John Bothwell, Rep. of William Bothwell,	Edward S Moyne,	Drumgoni and another
2549	Thomas Erskine,	Joseph P. O'Reilly,	Graham,
2550	James Mallet,	John C Wright,	Corbek,
2551	Patrick Sowey,	Sir Thomas N Leonard, Bart.	Annaghkilly,
2552	William Howey,	do.	Corranvanny,
2553	Alexander Nibloch and another	Mary Jane Nicholls and sons,	Anghnaslany,
2554	Francis Hughes,	Earl of Dartrey,	Doohin,
2555	Philip McNelly,	Miss S Reed,	Cashtern,
2556	William Ford,	Stewart Young and others,	Corravockin,
2557	George Chalew,	Dacre Hamilton,	Tenn,
2558	James Coogan, sender,	Mrs. Elizabeth Smith,	Corkalacka,
2559	John McKeowey,	Albert Medley and others,	Drumgor,
2560	Michael Fitzpatrick,	Miss Sarah Mahhink,	Gartytown,
2561	Francis Hoyten,	do.	Lisbrennkere,
			Total,

COUNTY OF

No.			
6741	Robert Weods,	James Brown,	Drumlindowny,
6742	William Wickbow,	do.	Drummond,
6743	William Thompson,	do.	do.
6744	James Barr,	do.	do.
6745	Joseph Henderson,	do.	do.
6746	John Karr,	do.	do.
6747	Mary Hughes, Rep. of John Hughes,	do.	Lisbunavany,
6748	Robert Whittle,	do.	Ballymackilgott,
6749	Michael Mallon,	do.	do.
6750	John Meehle,	do.	Annagh,

A. R. P.	£ s. d.	£ s. d.	£ s. d.		£ s. d.	£ s.
8 3 18	10 10 0	13 19 6	10 10 0			
1 1 0	5 0 0	6 2 5	6 6 0			
2 2 24	0 15 9	1 16 0	1 4 0			
41 1 4	20 15 0	15 5 7	18 5 3			
15 7 11	13 15 0	14 12 6	8 5 0			
10 1 15	7 10 0	4 0 4	6 0 0			
17 3 10	20 0 0	21 0 0	16 0 0			
13 7 6	14 15 0	13 3 10	11 5 0	Rent charged in 1838 from . . . 10 1 9		
14 2 34	uncertained	6 13 5	6 10 0			
10 0 33	9 15 0	10 0 0	8 10 0	1577	9 15 6
10 2 3	5 10 0	6 6 1	7 0 0			
6 1 20	5 0 0	3 14 11	8 0 0			
13 1 20	15 5 0	16 0 0	11 0 0	1804	10 10 0
5 1 20	2 15 0	6 3 1	8 6 0			
24 1 6	16 5 0	16 5 10	11 15 0			
15 7 10	13 15 0	11 0 6	11 0 0			
1 6 21	uncertained	1 19 5	8 10 0	1563	4 1 0
17 7 33	13 10 0	17 19 9	10 10 0			
9 2 20	7 10 0	7 15 6	6 0 0	1673	7 10 0
8 7 10	5 10 0	5 15 6	6 15 0			
272 2 16	189 10 0½	219 3 0½	162 13 3			

TYRONE.

5 0 19	4 10 0	4 7 6	3 15 0	
30 0 11	29 10 0	30 1 6	34 15 0	
3 3 15	3 0 0	5 15 6	3 0 0	
25 1 0	23 15 0	23 9 0	21 0 0	
16 3 6	14 15 0	18 11 0	14 15 0	
15 3 20	11 10 0	16 5 0	11 0 0	
22 1 26	19 0 0	20 17 6	17 0 0	
3 3 30	1 0 0	6 15 0	1 1 0	
10 0 0	10 15 0	11 15 0	8 15 0	
17 2 4	11 5 0	20 0 0	23 0 0	

Names of Assistant Commissioners by whom County was divided.	No.	Name of Tenant.	Name of Landlord.	Townland.
Assistant Commissioners— E. Green (Legal). J. Golden. J. P. Boswell.	6751	John Madole,	James Brown,	Texpymallep,
	6752	Edward Hughes,	do.	Drumny,
	6753	Robert Whelan,	do.	do.
	6754	Do.	do.	Derryfubble,
	6755	James Hughes,	do.	Carrus,
	6756	Mary Anne Hutchinson,	do.	Lyurla,
	6757	Archibald McGahey,	do.	Currowing,
	6758	Patrick McNally,	do.	Managers,
	6759	Henry Mallon,	do.	Gortshown,
	6760	Patrick Conoley,	do.	Drumintassh,
	6761	Bernard Mallon,	do.	Broughderreg,
	6762	Mayls Ward,	do.	Drumgahid,
	6763	Jane Raffery, Rep. of Peter Raffery,	do.	Gurretstown,
	6764	John Mallon,	do.	do.
	6765	James Watt,	do.	Lisbaulenagigh,
	6766	Patrick Shields,	do.	do.
	6767	Catherine McCrory,	do.	Stilloga,
	6768	Sarah McClure,	A. E. Daniel,	Cakenenn,
	6769	John McVey,	A. R. G. Moore,	Mullaghglass,
	6770	Martha Morris,	John Little,	Drummangallion,
	6771	Thomas Black,	Robert Wm. Lowry,	Killey,
	6772	Robert Gilmore,	Henry R. H. Stewart,	Knockraven,
	6773	Cornelius McCourt,	Hampton V. Morrow,	Drummond,
	6774	Owen Malley,	Rev. J. M. Beresford and another, Trustees of Commons of Castlestreet,	Inchaquoyn,
	6775	George Gilmore,	do.	Drum,
	6776	Bernard McGrath,	Commissioners of Education in Ireland,	Derrylughan,
	6777	Patrick Canavan,	do.	Aughnachoo,
	6778	Peter Canavan,	do.	do.
	6779	Henry Johnson,	Hugh McConkin,	Cookstorn,
	6780	William McGahey,	do.	do.
	6781	Robert Woods,	do.	do.
	6782	Jane Watt,	Colonel F. G. Mansfield,	Aughnackon,
	6783	Bernard Hughes,	do.	Jaffelly,
	6784	John McHugh,	Miss G. Crokrow,	Lagan,
	6785	Do.	do.	do.

Extent of Holding	Poor Law Valuation	Former Rent	Judicial Rent	Observations	Value of Tenancy
a. r. p.	£ s d	£ s. d.	£ s d		£ s d
17 1 6	9 10 0	10 16 6	9 0 0		
9 1 5	4 0 0	8 11 10	7 0 0		
6 0 1	1 13 0	5 10 0	3 4 6		
6 2 17	1 15 0	0 12 6	0 15 6		
17 3 16	13 10 9	18 15 0	13 15 0		
8 1 31	1 0 0	5 16 0	3 0 0		
13 1 7	10 10 0	13 0 0	10 5 0		
5 3 15	3 15 6	4 18 4	3 10 6		
18 1 6	13 10 9	15 10 6	10 10 0		
17 3 36	11 5 6	16 11 4	10 0 0		
8 1 30	6 13 0	9 10 0	7 7 6		
11 3 19	8 10 0	9 17 6	8 6 0		
6 3 30	4 5 0	6 16 0	6 10 0		
6 3 3	6 10 0	1 8 0	3 16 0		
10 1 33	8 10 0	8 15 0	7 10 0		
8 1 53	7 10 0	6 5 0	7 0 0		
10 1 33	9 0 6	10 1 0	8 6 0		
48 8 10	28 0 6	44 1 10	36 0 0		
13 1 0	11 13 6	13 6 6	10 16 0		
5 3 30	6 15 0	10 0 0	5 10 0		
60 1 5	11 0 0	17 11 8	10 0 0		
16 3 31	11 13 0	73 0 0	14 6 0		
10 3 0	9 3 0	12 6 10½	7 13 0		
31 0 0	3 0 0	3 0 0	7 0 0		
24 1 10	14 5 0	16 19 8	10 13 0		
27 3 31	1 15 0	6 10 0	4 6 0		
7 3 27	6 10 0	6 10 6	5 3 0		

Names of Absentee Proprietors by whom Conveyance desired.	No.	Name of Tenant.	Name of Landlord.	Townland.
Absentee Commissioners— E. Orme (Legal). J. Golding. J. P. Benyman.				
	4786	Bernard McTiernay,	Earl of Charlemont,	Killyfan,
	4787	Ellen Donnelly,	do.	do.
	4788	Patrick Hackett,	do.	Castlecarry,
	4789	Catherine Skeffington,	do.	do.
	4790	John Skeffington, Rep. of Anne Skeffington	do.	Legaliss,
	4791	James Gilhespie,	do.	Annaghmakown,
	4792	Do.,	do.	Fumlagh,
	4793	Patrick Horan,	Thomas F. Orror and others,	Garvetney,
	4794	John McGran,	U. P. Brackenridge, a minor, by Mrs M. A. Brackenridge	Lissanoughry,
	4795	James Farrell,	Sir John M Stewart, Bart,	Kinnataurny, Meolah,
	4796	John Hunter,	FitzAusten M. Armbriell,	Mullans,
	4797	Anne Gillan,	F. A. M. Moore and another,	Clonroe,
	4798	Thomas Curren,	Sir John Reabury, Bart,	Derryday,
	4799	Thomas Orr,	John C. Harris,	Somin,
	4800	Francis Donnelly,	Patrick Early,	Clonolly,
	4801	Michael Campbell,	James S. Cockran,	Alielaghile,
	4802	Patrick Campbell,	do.	do.
	4803	John Conlan,	do.	do.
	4804	Do.,	do.	do.
	4805	John Montague,	do.	do.
	4806	Peter Kelly,	do.	do.
	4807	Peter Heagney,	Francis P. Gervais,	Cormonny,
	4808	Hen Campbell,	do.	Dunnaggan,
	4809	Bridget Hart,	do.	Frraughanlevan,
	4810	James McConnell,	Mountroy Gladstone,	Ballymenna,
	4811	Francis McConnell,	do.	do.
	4812	David Dorran,	Major General A. G. M. Metres,	Cavan Kilgrean,
	4813	William Beatty,	do.	do.
	4814	Do.,	do.	Sky,
	4815	Owen McClaughey,	U. P. Brackenridge, a minor, by Mrs M. A. Brackenridge	Lismore,
	4816	Samuel McAtter,	Lord Charlemont,	Renkmore,
				Total,

7	3	15	3	5	6	6	5	2	6	10	0
16	2	22	5	0	6	7	9	11	6	10	6
17	2	0	16	15	2	14	15	2	19	5	6
5	3	1	5	0	0	5	11	0	2	16	0
80	1	5	81	0	0	23	18	6	16	14	0
18	3	13	40	0	0	56	1	10	43	0	0
11	2	5	10	5	0	10	10	0	7	13	0
14	1	12	11	0	0	13	0	0	9	0	6
22	1	16	17	0	0	15	0	0	18	10	0
5	2	32	6	10	0	6	5	0	6	0	0
13	0	0	5	5	0	8	12	6	7	1	0
5	0	5	5	13	0	5	0	6	6	0	0
11	3	5	5	0	0	7	13	6	5	18	0
67	0	0	10	10	0	10	13	3	7	16	0
134	0	0	11	0	0	21	10	7	17	15	0
5	0	25				5	15	7	5	7	0
13	1	21				6	5	2	6	5	7
13	3	5	5	3	0	7	16	10	5	10	0
16	0	0	5	5	0	7	14	10	6	19	0
6	2	20	4	0	0	5	10	0	5	7	0
21	3	10	5	5	0	16	0	0	7	5	0
19	2	10	11	0	0	16	10	0	6	0	0
25	3	20	6	0	0	5	5	0	6	10	0
13	3	20	6	0	0	5	5	0	6	10	0
12	0	0	5	0	0	5	5	2	6	16	0
7	3	0	5	5	0	5	15	10	6	10	0
6	2	0	4	0	0	5	0	0	3	10	0
70	5	10	18	10	0	15	5	1½	15	0	0
13	3	6	11	5	0	10	5	6	5	5	0
453	3	7	545	17	3	956	0	0	746	14	6

E. Esquire, &c. (Legal). J. M. Ware.	833	Patrick Cleary,	Anne Roacke and others, Guardians of Roacke, and the James Langrishe, Bart.,	Shropstown,
	834	Anastasia Only,	do.	Ballybraen,
	835	Michael M'Donald,	Colonel T St G. Caulfield,	Garraghurragh,
	836	Bridget Delahunty,	Joseph Greene and others, Trustees of Will of John Finn	Curraghmartin,
	837	Thomas Delahunty,	do.	do.
	838	Walter Phelan,	do.	Aglish, North,
	839	Edmund Dunphy,	do.	Curraghmartin,
	840	Catherine Delahunty,	do.	do.
	841	Elizabeth Cleary,	Anne Roacke and others, Guardians of Roacke, instant.	Shropstown,
	842	Ellen Byrne,	do.	do.
	843	Thomas Kennedy, Adm. of Michael Ryan.	Marquis of Ormonde,	Garryvoe M'Ad... devr.
	844	Do.,	do.	Killossery,
	845	Richard Shortall,	Formerly William Moore,	Ballybrae,
	846	John Murphy,	do.	Ballyhale,
				Total,

LEINSTER.

KILKENNY.

Share of Bridge Money	Poor Law Valuation	Former Rate	Interest Due	Observations	Point of Twenty
£. s. p.	£ s. d.	£ s. d.	£ s. d.		£ s. d.
17 0 12	64 10 0	74 18 4	54 0 0		
13 2 17	19 0 0	14 10 0	12 10 0		
66 1 14	54 10 0	62 13 8	52 0 0		
8 3 22	6 10 0	9 3 0	6 5 0		
16 3 10	26 0 0	24 0 0	20 0 0		
38 0 33	43 0 0	14 14 8	40 0 4		
53 2 16	20 0 0	84 5 5	62 0 0		
19 1 37	27 0 0	24 0 0	30 0 0		
36 0 27	32 0 0	47 14 4	40 0 0		
23 0 3	19 0 0	17 10 0	18 0 0		
66 1 27	61 5 0	60 0 0	56 0 0		
108 1 5	58 0 0	105 15 4	105 16 4		
115 0 0	65 0 0	90 15 0	65 0 0		
25 3 13	30 5 0	42 0 0	31 0 0		
85 3 16	30 0 0	43 0 0	31 10 0		
749 0 3	662 5 0	698 0 0	538 1 4		

COUNTY.

53 1 10	31 1 0	37 5 0	27 5 0		
6 1 30	3 10 0	6 0 0	4 0 0		
23 0 0	11 15 0	14 17 5	15 0 0		
28 1 24	13 13 0	16 10 0	12 0 0		
126 4 0	61 10 0	82 0 0	61 0 0		
108 2 0	46 0 0	51 0 0	48 0 0		
80 1 13	10 78 0	16 0 0	16 0 0		
34 2 4	11 16 0	11 0 0	9 0 0		
31 3 8	16 5 0	16 0 0	16 0 0		
50 1 0	13 15 0	25 0 0	11 0 0		

KING'S

Names of Assistant Commissioners by whom Cases were decided	No.	Name of Tenant	Name of Landlord	Townland
Assistant Commissioners—				
R. Reeves, q.c. (Legal). T. Ballard. J. M. Wann.	915	Michael Fagran,	Joseph Melvin, ...	...
	916	James Murray,	Joseph Reynolds,	...
	917	John Dunne, senior,	Sir Edward Croften, Bart., and another,	...
	918	Peggy Dunne,	do.	...
	919	John Dunne, junior,	do.	...
	920	Kieran, Geghlan,	Captain E. W. William,	...
				Total,

COUNTY OF

Assistant Commissioners—				
R. Reeves q.c. (Legal). T. Ballard. J. M. Wann.	1010	Edward McGivaney,	A. W. D Greville,	...
	1011	William Brabazon,	do.	...
	1012	Andrew Murphy,	Lord Longford,	...
	1013	Michael Farrell,	Ralph V. Leycester & another,	...
				Total,

QUEEN'S

Assistant Commissioners—				
R. Reeves, q.c (Legal). T. Ballard. J. M. Wann.	971	James Carroll,	Rev. B Fitzgerald,	...
	972	John Higgins,	Richard E Odlum,	...
	973	Pats Keenan,	Rev. James Fisher, Trustee of Land Cases	...
	974	Thomas Dollard,	do.	...
	975	Philip Cahill,	do.	...
	976	Michael Keenan,	Walterhouse Drought,	...
	977	James Spencer,	do.	...
	978	Cornelius Dowling,	Joseph Clarke,	...
	979	James Downey,	John Dempsey,	...
	980	Abraham Bloomfield,	Mrs Mary Clarke,	...
	981	John Dowling,	Oswald Adair,	...
	982	John Dolan,	Rev. William Pam,	...
	983	John King,	Lord Castletown,	...
	984	William Daniel,	Charles Holmes,	...
	985	William Sothern & exrs. of Geo. Sothern.	Thomas H. Harte,	...

COUNTY—*continued.*

Extent of Holding Acres	Poor Law Valuation	Former Rent	Judicial Rent	Observations	Value of Tenancy
A. R. P.	£ s. d.	£ s. d.	£ s. d.		£ s. d.
10 1 35	31 0 0	35 15 0	27 10 0		
1 2 7	3 0 0	4 15 0	1 0 0		
29 1 25	42 15 0	25 1 0	10 0 0		
3 1 29	2 0 0	1 0 0	1 10 0		
24 3 2	30 0 0	14 0 0	24 0 0		
21 0 0	9 5 0	9 10 0	7 15 0	By consent.	
669 1 30	347 1 0	371 1 3	320 0 0		

LONGFORD.

63 3 34	51 0 0	53 0 0	43 0 0		
144 2 11	163 5 0	183 15 6	150 0 0		
46 1 10	54 10 0	30 0 0	27 10 0		
19 1 29	9 10 0	13 6 3	8 0 0		
263 2 37	247 5 0	278 1 6	228 10 0		

COUNTY.

1 0 35	1 10 0	2 10 0	1 10 0		
45 3 24	37 0 0	44 0 0	56 0 0		
19 3 19	11 10 0	11 5 7	7 0 0		
31 3 1	12 0 0	13 10 0	9 0 0		
94 1 32	15 5 0	15 8 6	10 10 0		
3 3 6	3 15 0	7 0 0	4 0 0		
3 0 33	3 10 0	6 0 0	3 10 0		
40 0 0	11 10 0	20 0 0	14 10 0		
1 3 36	3 0 0	4 10 0	3 0 0		
37 3 23	23 10 0	34 15 0	19 0 0		
10 3 1	6 5 0	13 13 0	8 0 0		
10 3 0	9 0 0	12 0 0	9 10 0		
21 3 30	11 5 0	21 15 9	18 10 0		
1 1 15	1 5 0	6 0 0	1 5 0		
178 0 33	105 5 0	183 15 10	137 10 0		

Names of Assistant Commissioners by whom Case was decided	No.	Name of Tenant	Name of Landlord	Townland
Assistant Commissioners—				
R. Reeves, q c. (Legal)	886	Kyran Moore,	Roger Roberts,	Harristown,
T. Baldwin	887	Patrick Clooney,	Mary Oxyer,	Franisela,
J. M. Weir	888	Mary Anne Byrne,	John Orrom,	Crangerommaben,
	889	John Cullinan,	Mrs. Oua Mangan,	Garraghbeer,
	890	Denis Gorman,	Rev. William Lynan,	Derrivalla,
	891	Timothy Rourke,	do.	do
	892	James Murphy,	do.	do
	893	Lawrence Morris,	Thomas Kennah,	Brittas,
	894	Peter Dowling,	do.	Steuben,
	895	Anne McDonald,	Captain Ouby,	Dexingan,
	896	Patrick Fitzpatrick,	do.	do.
	897	Do.	do.	Beranger Mealy,
	898	Thomas Donnelly,	do.	Knockford & east,
	899	Michael Doyle, Rep. of Michael McClus,	do.	Bawnogganealy,
				Total,

Names of Assistant Commissioners	No.	Name of Tenant	Name of Landlord	Townland
Assistant Commissioners—				
R. Reeves, q n (Legal)	1082	George W Carr,	Rev. Nasman Dati,	Cronin,
J. M. Weir,	1083	John Cavard,	James Day Dauk,	Coolra,
T. Baldwin.	1084	John Conroy,	do	do
	1085	Patrick Clancy, Exec of James Clancy,	Frazer A. Leigh,	Harbingeraugh,
	1086	Thomas A Shannon, Admr of Pat Shannon	do.	Newtown,
	1087	Patrick H Barton,	Standish De C O'Grady and others	Mileown,
	1088	Arthur Murphy,	do	Ballintogga,
	1089	Edward Power,	do.	do
	1090	Hugh Connors,	H. G. Haughton,	Rathminor,
	1091	William Haughton,	do.	do,
	1092	Lawrence Turney,	do.	do.
	1093	Thomas Larkin,	do.	do.
	1094	Martin Shea,	Patrick E. Barton,	Heartwood,
	1095	John Forster,	Lofton A. Byrne, a minor, by Rev. P. Foley, his Guardian.	Clonard,
	1096	James Barker,	Matilda A. E Seagrave,	Ballybet,

COUNTY—continued.

Extent of Holding Statute	Army Lire Valuation	Former Rent	Judicial Rent	Observations	Value of Tenancy
A. R. P.	£ s. d.	£ s. d.	£ s. d.		£ s. d.
7 1 7	3 5 0	6 0 0	1 0 0		
5 1 0	3 15 0	7 0 0	3 15 0		
40 1 23	38 0 0	79 8 4	64 0 0		
34 3 3	31 10 0	40 0 0	35 10 0		
3 0 30	uncertain land	6 0 0	5 3 0		
30 1 11	30 10 0	37 0 0	15 10 0		
4 3 30	5 2 0	10 0 0	4 10 0		
41 3 0	21 10 0	36 10 9	20 0 0		230 0 0
43 1 6	34 0 0	37 10 6	23 10 0		400 0 0
40 7 0	77 0 0	84 14 0	30 0 0		
39 3 13	15 0 0	36 0 0	14 10 0		
41 1 6	16 3 0	28 0 0	21 10 0		
70 3 3	23 15 0	49 7 10	31 5 0		
43 0 23	34 10 0	80 10 0	22 10 0		
935 1 16	546 15 0	579 10 4	611 10 0		

WEXFORD.

100 2 13	17 15 0	110 0 0	50 0 0	By consent.	
15 1 3	5 0 0	11 0 0	5 0 0		
37 1 23	77 0 0	35 0 0	30 0 0		
79 1 36	43 10 0	73 10 0	12 0 0		
60 0 7	19 0 0	75 10 0	55 0 0		
80 3 10	34 0 0	40 0 0	33 0 0		
70 1 33	37 0 0	37 18 0	34 10 0		
71 1 2	36 0 0	33 8 0	36 10 0		
13 0 23	7 10 0	14 0 0	7 10 0		
5 0 30	1 0 0	4 0 0	8 10 0		
10 3 23	3 15 0	7 0 0	5 16 0		
6 1 30	4 10 0	8 3 0	5 6 0		
71 1 6	37 0 0	30 0 0	18 15 0		
4 13 1	3 0 0	3 0 3	6 6 0		
30 3 30	53 10 0	16 13 3	33 0 0		

Name of Assistant Commissioners by whom Cases were decided.	No.	Name of Tenant.	Name of Landlord.	Townland.
Assistant Commissioners—				
B. Reeves, Q.C. (Legal), J. M. Will, T. Baldwin.	1097	John Fitzhenry and another,	Matilda A. K. Seagrave, ..	Ballytarlly, ...
	1098	Johnson Ryan, ..	Edward Ferguson, ..	Malmayne, ...
	1099	James Gandon, ...	Michael B. Swettihome,	Ballinsloy, Lower,
				Total —

Assistant Commissioners—	No.	Name of Tenant.	Name of Landlord.	Townland.
Ulick Reeves (Legal), R. Arterin, C. O'Keeve.	4409	William Feeney, ...	Francis L. Ormyn, ...	Kmark, —
	4410	Margaret O'Donnell, ...	Bishop, minors, by Mrs. E. Towell, their guardian,	Ballinahinea,
	4411	Timly Geraghty, ...	George McKenna, ...	Clostmorogh, ...
	4412	Thomas Lyons, ...	do.	..	...	do.	...
	4413	Laurence Doher, ...	do.	...	...	do.	..
	4414	Patrick Fleming, ...	do.	...	...	do.	.
	4415	Thomas Concannon, —	do.	...	...	do.	...
	4416	Michael Heslar, ...	do.	...	..	do.	—
	4417	Martin Healy, ..	do.	.	...	do.	..
	4418	Thomas Babbit, ...	do.	...	...	do.	...
	4419	Pat Concannon, ...	do.	...	...	do.	...
	4420	Martin Concannon, ...	do.	...	...	do.	...
	4421	Mark Deien, —	do.	...	—	do.	...
	4422	Thomas Rodkin, —	do.	...	...	do.	...
	4423	Thomas White, ...	do.	...	...	do.	...
	4424	Mary Doolan, .	do.	...	—	do.	...
	4425	Patrick Quinn, ...	do.	...	...	do.	...
	4426	Bartore O'Byrne, ...	Richard Berridge, ...	Clynagh, .
	4477	Patrick Fahn, ...	Bishop, minors, by Mrs. E. Towell, their guardian.	Ballinahines, ...
	4428	Myles Chatellor, ...	do.	...	...	do.	...
				Total, ...

WEXFORD—*continued.*

Extent of Holding Statute	Poor Law Valuation	Rackrent Rent	Judicial Rent	Observations	Value of Tenancy
A. R. P.	£ s. d	£ s. d	£ s. d		£ s. d
33 3 35	43 0 0	43 14 10	46 0 0		
6 3 0	1 3 0	7 0 0	6 10 0		
37 0 13	18 10 0	16 0 0	18 10 0		
736 2 37	468 10 0	646 5 9	625 16 0		

CONNAUGHT.

GALWAY.

6 1 63	3 5 0	4 10 0	8 10 0		
11 0 23	5 0 0	7 10 0	5 0 0		
17 2 6	6 11 0	10 10 0	5 15 0		
6 1 18	3 3 0	3 10 0	3 10 0		
77 3 8	6 0 0	11 0 0	8 10 0		
15 3 3	3 0 0	6 10 0	6 0 0		
11 1 29	4 0 0	6 5 0	1 10 0		
17 3 36	4 10 0	7 0 6	8 10 0		
50 1 36	5 0 0	5 10 0	5 13 0		
14 3 21	6 0 0	6 15 0	4 10 0		
16 3 34	6 0 0	7 0 0	6 17 6		
11 2 37	3 0 0	4 10 0	3 5 0		
71 1 0	5 5 0	8 10 0	6 5 0		
17 0 9	6 15 0	9 0 0	6 15 0		
3 0 36	2 5 0	3 0 0	2 7 6		
71 1 17	3 15 0	8 10 0	5 0 0		
5 0 5	2 15 0	3 10 0	3 17 6		
9 0 0	4 15 0	10 0 0	4 10 0		
20 3 17	5 0 0	7 10 0	6 0 0		
17 3 9	3 0 0	5 0 0	8 13 0		
783 0 35	90 20 0	140 10 0	96 17 6		

Name of Assistant Commissioners by whom Cases were decided.	No.	Name of Tenant.	Name of Landlord.	Townland.
Assistant Commissioners—				
URBAN BOYTON (Legal). R. SPROULE.	2872	James M'Evoy,	John M Clements,	Gortnalficrt,
	2873	Patrick Travers,	George Lane Fox,	Pawn,
	2874	Michael Murphy,	do	Legavakeen,
	2875	Michael Clarke,	do	Birchhill,
	2876	James McPartland,	do	Mullagh,
	2877	Mary Flanagan, junr.,	do	Birchhill,
	2878	Margaret McGlInnon,	A. L. Tottenham,	Killtyrloghtor,
	2879	Henry McLoughlin,	A M. Crofton,	Drumboy,
	2880	John Doherty,	W. C B. Hawkers,	Knocknadlea,
	2881	Margaret McTeague,	William LaTouche,	Moyan,
	2882	M. J. Hines,	Arthur Maguire,	Drumkeeldin Glebe,
	2883	Bryan Maguveran,	Jane L Atkinson and others,	Greenockilla,
	2884	Anne Rourke,	Owen R. Blacks,	Grangemadarn,
	2885	Mathew Earl,	Lord Alfraswick,	Glenagh,
	2886	John Kinnan,	James O Lawdor,	Aughnavrin,
	2887	Judith Noblos,	do	do
	2888	Catherine Kearney,	do	do
	2889	Thomas Abbott,	do	Cardiff,
	2890	Catherine Dolan,	William Johnston,	Drumanger,
	2891	Owen Kelly,	Henry W S. Montgomery,	Carrigh,
	2892	Owen Hurpadla,	do	do
	2893	George R. Canby,	Owen Wynne,	Cloonloughor,
	2894	Mary Chrissy (widow),	Robert Hamilton,	Derrieville,
	2895	Michael Gallagher,	George L Fox,	Birchhill Barn,
	2896	Ellen Kelly, ...	do	Legavakeen,
	2897	John Curran,	do	Birchhill Barn,
	2898	Catherine Graham,	do	do
	2899	Catherine Hamilton,	do	Tullysunorary,
	2900	Bernard McHugh,	do	Kilnamaken,
				Total,

LEITRIM.

Extent of Holding Statute	Poor Law Valuation	Former Rent	Judicial Rent	Observations	Value of Tenancy
A. R. P.	£ s. d.	£ s. d.	£ s. d.		£ s. d.
27 0 12	5 15 0	3 10 0	3 10 0	By consent	
20 3 8	8 12 0	2 0 0	3 5 0	do.	
28 2 0	8 5 0	1 10 0	5 0 0	do.	
18 2 12	1 13 0	1 13 0	2 17 6	do.	
27 1 3	2 10 0	1 10 0	2 2 0	do	
16 1 13	1 13 0	1 13 0	2 0 0	do	
13 1 35	1 10 0	4 6 0	1 13 0	do	
13 1 21	6 15 0	8 13 6	7 13 0	do	
7 3 25	4 13 0	6 0 0	4 13 0		
31 0 0	15 0 0	10 10 0	17 0 0		
36 1 0	12 0 0	17 15 6	13 10 0		£ s. d.
53 3 15	on acceptance	5 0 0	3 5 0	Rent charged in 1871 from .　.　. 3 0 0	
16 1 6½	3 13 0	10 10 0	8 0 0		
11 0 1	2 15 0	5 10 0	4 10 0		
17 2 0	5 15 0	7 0 0	3 15 0		
17 3 10	8 18 0	7 0 0	6 6 0		
30 1 51	3 0 0	8 0 0	6 0 0		
27 1 10	13 0 0	16 0 0	13 0 0		
11 0 31	4 13 0	1 4 0	3 10 0		
20 0 0	7 0 0	11 0 0	7 10 0		
16 0 37	4 0 0	7 0 0	4 10 0		
134 0 3	140 13 0	163 5 0	111 0 0		
7 0 23	2 15 0	1 5 0	2 15 0		
11 0 18	3 5 0	3 0 0	3 0 0		
31 0 1	5 15 0	3 0 0	4 6 0		
2 1 11	1 15 0	1 0 0	1 10 0		
40 1 58	3 13 0	3 0 0	1 5 0		
5 0 20	2 10 0	1 1 0	2 10 0		
18 1 0	3 0 0	3 0 0	8 10 0		
915 2 27½	299 3 0	225 13 0	296 13 6		

6868	Michael Kennisey,	do	
6869	Michael Feldon	M. A. Logan and smith	
6870	Patrick Grady,	do	
6871	James King,	do	
6872	James Connoll,	do	
6873	Mary Kenna,	do	
6874	Pat Grady (Tom),	do	
6875	Bartholomew Turpey,	Mrs Margaret O'Gorman	
6876	Pat. Caswell,	do	
6877	Ellen Daffy,	do	
6878	James Philips,	do	
6879	Mary Marren,	do	
6880	Bridget Hanebury,	do	
6881	Catherine Owens,	do	
6882	Patrick Judge,	do	
6883	John Robinson,	do	

MAYO.

Extent of Holding Statute	Poor Law Valuation	Former Rent	Judicial Rent	Change since		Value of Tenancy
A. R. P.	£ s. d.	£ s. d.	£ s. d.		£ s. d.	£ s. d.
16 1 15	19 5 0	16 0 0	18 10 0			
10 2 8	13 8 0	11 0 0	13 0 0	Rent changed in 1877 from . . .	10 0 0	
8 0 0	1 17 0	3 6 6	2 3 0	By consent		
6 7 0	7 6 0	9 3 0	7 10 0	do		
18 3 6	9 0 0	7 10 0	6 0 0			
1 9 20	1 2 6	2 6 8	1 16 0			
6 2 28	1 18 0	5 20 0	2 10 0			
16 2 7	1 16 0	3 0 0	2 0 0			
11 8 5	1 3 0	3 5 0	1 15 0			
6 0 27	1 2 6	2 10 0	2 10 0			
9 2 13	3 15 0	5 0 0	3 16 0			
13 3 0	6 0 0	8 5 8	1 5 0			
13 2 17	3 0 0	1 15 0	2 5 0	Rent changed in 1840 from, do	3 11 6 1 0 7	
26 3 13	4 15 0	6 6 0	4 10 0			
13 1 32	3 0 0	4 15 0	3 5 0			
19 0 1	3 1 0	6 10 0	3 5 0	do	3 0 0	
10 1 26	3 10 0	7 0 0	4 5 6			
18 2 35	1 10 0	3 0 0	2 7 6			
19 1 34	2 10 0	3 6 0	2 10 0	1871	1 19 4	
294 0 19	76 8 0	108 15 0	89 1 0			

ROSCOMMON.

7 5 30	9 15 0	6 5 9	5 5 0			
26 5 0	10 16 0	9 8 0	6 10 0			
30 3 3	19 0 0	21 0 0	17 0 0			
45 3 26	30 10 0	30 0 6	26 0 0	Rent changed in 1875 from, . . .	26 6 6	
43 0 0	25 10 0	30 6 0	29 0 0			
11 2 12	9 15 0	11 16 8	7 0 0			
7 0 6	6 16 0	8 0 0	4 10 0			
1 3 33	8 0 0	10 5 0	5 0 0	1875	7 0 0	
7 2 30	4 10 0	6 5 6	6 10 0	1885	6 3 0	
6 1 0	6 10 0	9 2 0	8 7 6			
20 3 17	11 10 0	13 10 0	10 10 0			

Name of Assistant Commissioner by whom Case was decided.	No.	Name of Tenant	Name of Landlord	Townland
Assistant Commissioners— ULICK BURKE (Legal). R. SPROULE.	2156	Lawrence McDonnell, ...	J. W. Talbot, ...	Clonnalade, ...
	2157	Michael Kelly, —	do. — —	do. —
	7138	Edward Connolly, —	do. — —.	do. —
	6269	William Ferny, —	do. — ...	do. —
	2340	William Tom, —	T. C. W. Sandford, ...	Ballynbromley,—
	2341	B. Tom, — ...	do. — —	do. ...
				Total, ...

Assistant Commissioners— F. C. Nonnen (Legal). J. G. Barry. J. Ryan.	2333	James Beverty, ..	James Collins and another, Reps. of R. P. Irwin.	Ragwood, .
	2339	John McDonagh, —	Robert Caddell, — ...	Dam,
	2340	James Brown, ...	do. ... —	Kilfree, —
	2341	Bartholomew Goff, —	do. ... —	Dam, —
	2342	Thomas O'Hara, —	do.	do. —
	2463	James Tansey, —	do. ... —	Rathmaddy, ..
	2011	Thomas O'Hara & many	do. — ...	Attongimen t, —
	2363	Thomas Proyne, ...	do. ... —	Dam, —
	2316	John McLoughlin ...	Col. E King Harman, ...	Cancooney, —
	2347	John Kearney, ..	Michael McHugH, .	Cancooney,
	2362	Patrick Hara, —	Edward Hawley, —	Rascaleystown, West ...
	2319	Michael McuUHan	A. French	Threeherobaine ..

A.	B.	P.	£	s.	d.	£	s.	d.	£	s.	d.		£	s.	d.	£	s.	d.
37	0	3	10	0	0	11	9	0	8	10	0	Rent changed in 1862						
79	0	65	10	0	0	10	0	0	8	10	0	from 4 16 0	4	16	0			
31	1	70	11	10	0	14	6	0	13	0	0	do.	4	16	0			
12	3	59	4	10	0	5	9	0	1	10	0							
37	0	0	19	10	0	23	8	8	19	10	0							
78	1	11	14	18	0	19	0	0	16	0	0							
306	3	11	108	13	0	337	17	8	189	18	6							

SLIGO.

19	1	19½	4	5	0	8	0	0	4	0	0							
18	0	39	6	3	0	6	11	0	3	3	0							
37	0	81	10	8	0	10	8	0	9	8	8	Rent changed in 1862						
30	3	6	5	10	0	8	3	0	5	0	0	from 11 6 0	11	6	0			
16	3	27	6	18	0	7	2	9	8	0	0							
25	7	13	10	5	0	10	17	0	8	5	0							
94	1	46	15	8	0	14	13	6	13	0	0							
13	3	15	6	3	0	6	13	0	5	10	0							
31	1	31	8	10	0	3	14	0	8	13	6							
7	1	19	—			7	16	0	7	0	0							
17	0	0	6	0	0	10	3	6	7	0	0							
16	3	2	1	10	0	3	8	8	2	5	6		1870	8	3	4
13	1	20	1	10	0	10	3	0	7	0	0							
9	3	0	7	0	0	10	0	0	8	0	0	By consent						
11	9	17	58	0	0	33	5	0	36	10	0	do.						
6	3	31	6	3	0	Account settled.			5	15	0	do.						
33	1	3	33	10	0	28	8	6	83	5	0							
13	3	26	36	0	0	31	11	6	26	0	0							
13	3	38	30	10	0	25	10	6	21	10	0							
39	1	31	30	0	0	27	10	0	31	0	0							
31	1	9	78	10	0	74	6	10	20	15	0							

Browne,	...	Lord H
London,	...	Charles
Charleton,	.	Oderste
gan,		Robert
Foley,	..	Sir Ovli
Mahony,	.	Myles
D. Jackson,	..	Mrs A
Conlon,	..	Owen
O'Hara,	..	Uncl

SLIGO—*continued.*

Extent of D Allot Tenants	Poor Law Valuation	Pre-exg. Rent	Judicial Rent	Observations	Value of Tenancy
	£ s. d.	£ s. d.	£ s. d.	£ s. d.	£ s. d.
5? 2 13	5 0 0	13 10 0	9 0 0	Rent changed in 1838 from . 5 0 0	
33 1 10	14 1? 0	21 0 0	14 0 0		
0 3 6	—	2 10 0	1 0 0		
10 3 3	6 15 0	5 0 0	6 5 0		
61 3 1	11 5 0	13 10 0	11 10 0		
13 3 10	3 15 0	6 7 6	5 0 0		
43 3 23	9 10 0	11 15 0	9 0 0	1863 5 0 0	
279 1 20	23 14 0	33 13 8	37 0 0		
10 3 1	7 0 0	9 15 5	7 0 0		
161 3 3	34 0 0	45 0 0	28 10 0		
43 0 50	19 0 0	25 10 0	20 0 0		
14 3 30	12 5 6	16 12 11	13 10 0		
16 0 37	14 10 0	15 0 0	13 0 0		
7 3 3	6 6 0	6 5 0	6 5 0		
30 1 1	9 5 0	20 0 0	18 0 0		
17 3 33	62 0 0	63 0 0	38 0 0		
15 3 0	on area claimed	subject claimed	3 10 0		
33 3 3	25 10 0	31 0 0	18 5 5		
1,345 3 33	113 10 0	601 19 11	543 17 6		

MUNSTER.

CLARE.

25 3 14	11 0 0	75 0 0	33 0 0		
5 3 15	6 0 0	5 15 0	5 3 0		
4 0 35	1 15 0	5 0 0	5 0 0		
15 1 31	7 0 0	9 5 0	6 5 0		
61 0 0	6 15 0	6 6 0	7 5 0	By request	
31 0 0	13 0 0	15 5 0	14 0 0	do	
16 0 0	3 15 0	9 1 0	7 5 0		
7 0 0	5 5 0	5 6 11	6 7 5		
41 1 0	5 15 0	13 10 0	10 10 0		170 0 0
13 2 50	6 5 0	10 10 0	6 10 0		
36 7 30	5 15 0	10 10 0	6 10 0		

Lessees of Dairying Farms.	Poor Law Valuation	Former Rent	Judicial Rent	Glebe's value	Value of Tenancy
A. R. P.	£ s. d.	£ s. d.	£ s. d.		£ s. d.
80 3 5	11 5 0	11 0 0	10 0 0		
197 1 34	17 0 0	20 0 0	15 0 0		
75 0 0	5 0 0	14 0 0	7 0 0		
14 0 0	7 10 0	13 0 0	11 15 0		
8 0 0	5 0 0	8 7 6	4 15 0		
90 0 0	7 15 0	10 10 0	7 10 0		
5 0 7	2 10 0	4 0 0	3 0 0		
39 0 27	20 0 0	25 7 6	12 0 0		
165 1 10	93 15 0	111 17 7	90 0 0		
13 2 16	8 15 0	10 0 0	8 0 0		
11 3 17	5 15 0	7 9 4	5 15 0		
18 1 8	33 0 0	34 4 0	38 0 0		
69 2 34	37 15 0	50 0 0	40 0 0		
9 1 30	9 10 0	11 17 7	9 0 0		
313 3 4	161 10 0	233 14 0	177 10 0		
21 0 0	17 15 0	17 3 10	12 10 0		
171 0 16	15 10 0	25 10 0	20 0 0		
73 0 0	13 0 0	11 5 3	10 0 0		
25 1 15	11 10 0	13 2 2	10 0 0		
51 1 6	14 10 0	18 11 0	12 10 0		
6 3 11	4 5 0	7 7 0	4 15 0		
1 0 16	1 0 0	1 10 0	1 0 0		
3 0 35	1 10 0	3 10 0	3 0 0		
4 1 22	5 10 0	5 13 6	8 10 0		
22 1 25	10 10 0	21 4 8	17 0 0		
33 2 6	19 5 0	16 3 7	14 0 0		
8 1 20	5 10 0	6 4 7	4 0 0		
9 1 9	7 5 0	15 15 2	10 10 0		
29 3 31	5 0 0	6 10 4	4 10 0		
45 3 25	31 0 0	73 10 0	35 0 0		
34 3 37	27 15 0	29 3 3	21 0 0		
16 0 30	7 15 0	11 4 0	7 15 0		
39 1 25	41 15 0	61 1 7	71 10 0		
33 1 3	31 0 0	46 0 0	39 0 0		

Name of Assistant Commissioners by whom Court was divided.	No.	Name of Tenant.	Name of Landlord.
Assistant Commissioners —			
E. G. MacDermot (Legal). A. Ormsby. J. Cunningham.	2620	John O'Grady,	Madame A. de la Haye,
	2621	James Brown,	do
	2622	Thomas McGrath, Admr of Judith McGrath	William H Cusack and as Trustee of William G Jun. a minor.
	2623	Patrick McGrath, Admr of Judith McGrath	do
	2624	Honoria Cusack,	do
	2625	Margt Moylan, Admr of Wm Moylan	Arthur G Judd,
	2626	Timothy Closs, Junr,	do
	2627	Patrick Fahey, Admr of P. Fahey	Lieut Col. Edward Arenta
	2628	Mary Savage,	do
	2629	Daniel Byrne,	do
	2630	Michael Slattery,	do
	2631	Thomas Donnellan, Admr of Michael Donnellan	do
	2632	Ellen Brennan, Admr of Austin Brennan,	Marquis Conyngham,
	2633	Mary Finch,	do
	2634	Ellen Brennan, Admr of Austin Brennan	do
	2635	Thomas Connell,	do
	2636	Do	do
	2637	Michael Nihell,	Henry J. Moloney,
	2638	Thomas Rodgers, Admr of M. Rodgers	do
	2639	Mary Dundon,	do
	2640	Michael Moloney,	do
	2641	William Dundon,	do
	2642	Patrick Healy,	Col. Hon. Charles W Wh

CLARE—continued.

Amount of Existing Rent	Poor Law Valuation	Former Rent	Judicial Rent	Observations	Value of Tenantry
£ s. d	£ s. d	£ s. d	£ s. d		£ s. d
17 2 10	18 5 0	72 11 5	17 10 0		
30 0 6	23 0 0	38 0 0	25 0 0		
61 1 21	37 15 5	34 10 0	27 10 0		
40 6 10	31 10 6	41 1 0	37 10 0		
5 3 15	3 10 0	6 0 0	3 17 6		
10 1 0	8 10 0	12 7 1	9 0 0		
60 1 30	27 15 0	34 15 2	25 0 0		
27 3 0	9 8 0	9 5 0	6 15 0		
44 3 1	16 0 0	17 0 0	11 0 0		
27 3 0	9 0 0	5 5 0	7 0 0		
19 1 34	23 5 0	24 7 0	17 13 6		
15 3 81	7 10 0	6 10 0	6 10 0		
61 3 87	43 15 0	44 0 0	33 0 0		
69 1 33	87 0 0	108 0 0	76 0 0		
3 2 17	4 0 0	6 0 0	5 10 0		
18 0 0	6 10 0	12 0 0	8 15 0		
75 1 81	31 0 0	43 0 0	25 0 0		
5 3 0	1 5 0	3 5 4	2 0 0		
9 0 0	3 5 0	5 7 3	3 15 0		
7 3 0	2 5 0	4 8 2	3 0 0		
13 1 6	3 5 9	5 15 3	3 10 0		
5 0 0	1 16 0	3 4 7	2 2 0		
9 1 33	11 15 0	16 4 2	13 10 0		
150 3 0	30 0 0	50 6 0	40 0 0	Do. annual.	
28 3 8	7 15 0	10 0 0	10 0 0		50 0 0
1 0 5	1 5 0	7 10 0	5 14 3	do.	
1771 1 0	1,170 16 0	1,530 8 9	1,285 17 8		

Assistant Commissioners—

M. T. Grean (Legal).
J. Hardgrove
J J O'Hallorassy

9715	Samuel Brown, and anor.	Robert Leslie,	...	Tyrtaghe, Lower,
9716	Jeremiah Robbins,	St John T. B Douglas,		Tullabrrell,
9717	Robert G. Crothers,	do	...	Farranwen,
9718	John Dunpen,	Edward Stanley,	...	Ballynacorrha,
9719	Michael Costelloe,	Col. James Crosbie,	...	Letumore,
9720	Catherine Stack,	Charles H. Jones and others, Assignees of Daniel Shent, a Bankrupt,		Inchamagilrough,
9721	Elizabeth Ross,	Robert A. Finham,	...	Kilmore,
9722	Timothy Unrun,	John Folents and others,		Ballygarrett,
9723	Mary Buckley,	do	...	do
9724	Thomas Lyons and anor,	do	...	do
9725	John Sullivan,	Leslie Wren,		Carrignes,
9726	John O'Connor,	Thomas W. Sanien,		Gortroe Ballyhy,
9727	William Power,	Edward M Supple,		Cloonanalin,
9728	Nicholas Quilter,	do		Minterough,
9729	Cornelius McNamara,	Wilson Gun,		Guthard, South,
9730	Maurice Galvin, junior,	Lord Oranmhwaine,		Ballyrehan, West,
9731	Thomas McElligott,	do		Coolaclong,
9732	Thomas Flaherty,	Edward G Stokes,		Shehacross Stroban
9733	James Collins,	Mank C Irwin,		Monbeter,
9734	Margaret Hanrahan,	do		do
9735	Patrick Nolan,	Michael Morgan and another,	Mayfield,
9736	Daniel Foley,	do	...	Mayfield, North,
9737	Edmund E Hagen,	do		do
9738	David Uroton,	Charles Evans and others,	Mayfield, South,
9739	Michael Lynch,	Bartholomew O'C. Hargus and another	do
9740	Thomas Phillon,	George L Grimes,		Glashnaaram,
9741	Frank Murphy,	do		do
9742	Robert Mark,	Wilson Gun,		Tuppot, West

CORK.

Extent of Holding Statute.	Poor Law Valuation	Former Rent	Judicial Rent	Observations	Value of Tenancy
a. r. p.	£ s. d.	£ s. d.	£ s. d.		£ s. d.
13 0 35	9 10 0	13 17 0	13 10 0		

KERRY.

22 1 0	13 5 0	11 0 0	24 0 0		
299 0 0	12 10 0	34 10 5	27 0 0	By consent.	
713 3 36	114 15 0	200 0 0	150 0 0	Rent changed in 1875 from . . . 120 0 0	£ s. d.
53 0 16	10 10 0	20 0 0	16 0 0		
85 1 25	9 12 0	15 0 8	11 5 0	1869 18 5 8	
10 0 0	4 15 0	12 0 0	7 15 0		
75 5 13	51 5 0	67 0 0	91 0 0	1865 70 0 0	
7 3 0	1 15 0	2 0 0	3 0 0		
5 0 0	1 15 0	4 0 0	3 0 0		
73 1 18	28 0 0	63 3 4	40 0 0		
11 2 6	5 15 0	9 4 4	6 15 0		
140 1 18	77 10 0	70 0 0	47 0 0	1863 33 0 0	
60 3 13	4 15 0	30 0 0	11 0 0		
51 0 20	36 0 0	60 0 0	12 12 6		
64 2 24	53 0 0	50 0 0	40 0 0	1870 36 0 0	
47 8 18	23 0 0	11 0 0	34 0 0	1860 11 4 6	
16 0 0	7 5 0	11 0 0	8 0 0		
54 0 20	26 10 0	60 0 0	43 0 0	By consent.	
24 2 0	11 10 0	30 15 0	15 0 0	Rent changed in 1870 from . . . 15 10 0	
36 3 13	11 0 0	20 15 0	11 5 0		
2 1 6	1 15 0	2 16 8	3 0 0	By consent.	
51 1 8	16 10 0	34 0 0	18 7 0		
56 3 20	20 15 0	33 0 0	25 0 0		
23 1 34	8 15 0	16 0 0	11 0 0	Rent changed in 1867 from . . . 13 0 0	
16 2 23	5 0 0	14 4 8	10 16 0	1874 11 0 0	
31 1 6	7 0 0	16 0 0	8 0 0		
95 3 11	17 15 0	36 0 0	21 13 6	1854 40 0 0	
17 2 23	3 15 0	13 0 0	7 7 0		

Name of Assistant Commissioner by whom Case was decided	No.	Name of Tenant	Name of Landlord	Townland
Assistant Commissioners—				
M. T. Carey (Legal). J. Haughton, J. J. O'Shaughnessy.	7744	Robert Stack,	Wilson Gun,	Benmore, West,
	7746	Michael Harrington,	do.	Chippingtown,
	7745	John Harrington,	do.	do.
	7744	Thomas Walsh,	do.	do.
	7747	Michael Carroll,	do.	do.
	7748	Michael Walsh,	do.	do.
	7749	John Walsh,	do.	do.
	7720	Mathew Mahony,	do.	do.
	7721	Michael Gunter,	do.	do.
	7748	Patrick Kennelly,	Sir Maurice Fitzgerald, Bart,	Kean Lettoshore,
	7722	Patrick Costelloe,	Major Piumm Chute,	Tureigh,
	7721	Carroll Sullivan,	William Thompson,	Cahirwohikeen,
	2725	James O'Connor,	Maurice Dorn and another,	Ghaleargaahakeen,
	7726	Catherine Griffin & anor,	Venerable Archdeacon Denny,	Kerries, West,
	7727	Johanna Reale,	do.	do.
	7728	Denis Laler,	Sir Edward Denny, Bart,	Cloughmakibshore,
	1130	John Fitzgerald,	do.	Lismagten,
	7760	Thomas Moynihan,	Coleman Bateman,	Deeks,
	7761	Patrick Dowse,	Probus M. R. Bateman,	Ballinorig, East,
	7762	Mary O'Donnell,	J. J. Brown,	Duncannaflagh,
	7763	William A. O'Connor,	Rickard Oliver Oliver,	Drumkeen, West,
	7764	Edward Garralon,	do.	Ballyboniane,
	7761	Patrick McClash,	do.	Enticklwark,
	7766	John Halloran,	do.	Ballyhenlone,
	7767	Maurice Fitzgerald,	do.	do.
	7768	Philip Reddy,	Francis O. Post,	Rosheen,
	7769	John Brown,	Stephenson A. Blackwood and others,	Craughcrummeen,
	7770	Do.	do.	Dysart Marsh,
	7771	Hanora Dowling,	Ballinteeglow Lime Quarries Company (Limited),	Ballinteeglow,
	7772	Mary McCarthy,	do.	do.
	7773	Richard Qualter,	Daniel F. Supple and others,	Clonaslee,
	7774	John Laler,	William T. T. Crosbie,	Letsmore,
	7775	Daniel Hayes,	do.	Kanekangodsh,
	7776	John Burns,	do.	do.
	7777	George Lynch,	do.	Kanikwark,

KERRY—*continued.*

Extent of Holding &c.	Poor Law Valuation.	Former Rent.	Judicial Rent.	Observations.	Value of Tenancy.
A. r. p.	£ s. d.	£ s. d.	£ s. d.	£ s. d.	£ s. d.
41 3 20	8 0 0	16 8 0	14 4 0		
66 3 4	10 15 0	15 0 0	9 15 0		
28 2 4	10 15 0	13 0 0	9 15 0		
21 3 29	11 0 0	14 0 0	10 10 0		
36 0 26	13 5 0	17 0 0	13 10 0	Rent arranged in 1855	
66 0 36	11 0 0	14 0 0	10 10 0	from . , 8 0 0	
23 1 31	11 0 0	14 0 0	10 10 0		
21 3 13	10 10 0	14 0 0	11 0 0		
34 3 25	18 0 0	25 0 0	18 10 0		
49 2 2	28 10 0	36 0 0	32 0 0	1877 62 0 0	
11 3 9	20 5 0	50 0 0	34 0 0		
80 3 6	101 0 0	153 10 0	90 0 0		
12 1 38	2 10 0	1 0 0	7 0 0		
61 2 22	64 10 0	91 5 0	68 0 0		
31 3 0	57 5 0	76 5 0	57 10 0		
76 3 23	34 10 0	58 4 0	38 10 0		
31 3 26	10 11 0	31 17 9	11 10 0		
19 3 0	13 10 0	25 0 0	18 0 0	1887 23 10 0	
31 1 0	16 5 0	23 10 6	13 6 0		
31 1 16	24 5 0	32 0 0	24 12 6		
64 3 34	84 10 0	45 16 10	36 0 0		
36 3 21	17 0 0	36 0 0	21 10 6	1867 30 0 0	
157 0 0	62 15 0	104 0 0	86 0 0	1877 110 0 0	
42 3 26	29 0 0	43 0 0	33 0 0	1870 46 0 0	
42 2 16	14 16 0	10 0 0	27 0 0	do. 42 5 0	
3 0 2	1 5 0	4 0 0	3 0 0		
40 8 32	16 7 0	30 0 0	24 0 0		
8 2 29	2 5 0	6 0 0	4 4 0		
14 8 77	7 0 0	13 2 6	8 0 0		
26 8 77	7 0 0	12 6 8	8 0 0		
47 3 80	31 0 0	50 0 0	41 0 0	1856 11 10 0	
30 0 0	13 6 0	43 16 0	33 10 0		
30 0 0	11 15 0	22 0 6	18 15 0	1877 23 1 6	
31 0 32	7 15 0	23 7 2	14 3 0	1861 31 7 10	
87 3 33	7 15 0	29 3 6	18 0 0	1859 10 10 0	

IRISH LAND COMMISSION.

COUNTY OF

Name of Assistant Commissioners by whom Cases were decided	No.	Name of Tenant	Name of Landlord	Townland
Assistant Commissioners— M. T. Green (Legal). J. Havegreen. J. J. O'Shaughnessy.	3775	Timothy Griffin,	Arthur Newmarkstown,	Kilberry,
	3776	Peter Hill,	do.	Moran,
	3780	Terence O'Donnell,	do.	Lack, East,
	3781	Thomas Foley,	do.	Lack,
	3782	Thomas Jones,	Lord Ventry,	Knockahorn,
	3783	Michael Moore,	do.	Tullig,
	3784	Do.	do.	Graham,
	3785	John Sumner,	do.	Murraham,
	3786	Do.	do.	Cloghanabohane and another.
	7187	John O'Callaghan,	Michael Mulchinock,	Cloghers,
	3788	William Barrett,	Robert Day, by Mrs. Frances Day, his mother and next friend,	Kent Kerries,
				Total,

COUNTY OF

Assistant Commissioners—				
L. Doyle (Legal). T. Walpole. C. O'Keeffe.	2280	James Delany,	Honourable Charles White,	Poppintown,
	2281	John Maher,	do.	Williams,
	2282	Margaret Murray,	Henry Santeau,	Greenstown,
	2283	William O'Brien,	William E. Marshall,	Timahoe,
	2284	William Clifford,	Edward White,	Clonagheen,
	2285	Daniel M. Wallace,	Thomas Stewart,	Skeahally,
	2286	Thomas Hankels,	William Ollem,	Longfordpass,
	2287	John Haugh,	Joseph J. O'Flanagan,	Old Court,
	2288	John O'Brien,	William E. Marshall,	Kylemacarush,
	2289	William Carroll,	Earl of Normanton,	Martstown,
	2290	Malachy Ryan,	do.	Ballyroveen,
	2291	Do.	do.	do.
	2292	Jeremiah Quinlan,	do.	do.
	2293	William Neill and coys.	Valentine Ryan,	Ballyliveen,
	2294	James Greene,	Ambor J. Moore,	Ballinaglough,
				Total,

KERRY—continued.

Extent of Holding	Prev. Law Valuation	Former Rent	Judicial Rent	Observations	Value of Tenancy
A. R. P.	£ s. d.	£ s. d.	£ s. d.	£ s. d.	£ s. d.
97 1 11	50 5 0	76 0 0	40 0 0	Rent changed in 1876	
77 0 21	38 10 0	60 0 0	50 0 0	from — 60 0 0	
18 0 0	14 10 0	38 17 0	19 0 0	1880 45 1 8	
29 0 0	31 20 0	62 0 0	19 10 0	1887 11 0 0	
117 5 0	18 15 0	35 0 0	96 0 0		120 0 0
13 2 31	45 10 0	16 0 0	17 0 0		
3 2 36	1 10 0	2 10 0	1 18 0		
4 0 0	3 10 0	6 15 0	4 0 0		
13 0 16	3 0 6	4 4 0	2 5 0		
65 2 20	104 5 0	217 1 4	120 0 0		
61 3 31	98 0 0	143 16 10	114 0 0		
3,400 3 35	1,982 13 0	4,650 2 2	2,131 0 5		

TIPPERARY.

15 3 7	18 15 0	13 13 6	10 0 0		
34 1 14	11 10 0	11 0 6	9 10 0		
56 1 10	24 0 0	43 18 0	27 5 0		
114 3 28	42 0 0	71 8 8	44 0 0		
11 2 30	4 0 0	5 7 0	4 10 5		
115 0 0	67 15 0	55 0 0	45 0 0		
80 2 17	62 10 0	70 0 0	12 0 0		
3 0 12	1 15 0	4 10 0	3 0 0	By consent.
108 0 0	63 2 0	82 17 1	70 0 0	Provision has been made in this case
53 3 12	37 18 0	45 8 5	45 8 5	as regards a labourer.
37 1 20	41 15 0	54 7 8	45 0 0		
11 2 1	11 0 0	17 14 6	16 0 8		
45 1 35	81 0 0	64 8 4	55 0 0		
110 0 37	87 0 0	130 0 0	106 0 0		
139 3 23	175 5 0	277 1 2	272 1 2		
934 3 10	705 3 0	853 0 1	779 11 3		

COUNTY OF WATERFORD.

IRISH LAND COMMISSION.

No.	Name of Owner	Tenant's Name	Townland		Poor Law Valuation	Former Rent	Judicial Rent	Observations	Value of Tenancy £ s. d.
				£ s. d.	£ s. d.	£ s. d.	£ s. d.		
Amount of Judicial Rents fixed by Sub-Commissioners:—									
Adjourned Cases heard:—								By agreement	
L. Byrne (Legal)	831	John Power,	Mary O'Keefe,	Carrigateen,	23 8 0	32 0 0	52 10 0	65 0 0	
T. Walford,	845	Patrick Ahearne,	R. T. Usher,	Kinsalebeg,	15 3 35	11 0 0	14 0 0	8 10 0	
G. O'Keeffe	846	Michael Hholp,	Marquis of Waterford,	do.	12 1 8	9 0 0	8 10 0	6 10 0	
	847	Thos. Kiely,	Count de la Poer,	Kinsalebeg,	36 0 30	—	38 8 1	21 0 0	
	848	Quinn and Whelan,	H. F. Chearnley,	Portlaw,	179 2 23	28 8 0	37 0 0	38 20 0	
	849	Owen V. Kiely and others,	Herbert F. O'Dell and another, actions by Wm. O'Brien and others,	Shanbally,	50 0 28	33 13 0	38 14 4	20 0 0	
	950	Do.	do.	Lough,	57 3 20	23 10 0	36 1 30	31 0 0	
				Total —	121 3 25	147 10 0	254 5 1	183 10 0	

CIVIL BILL COURT.

SUMMARY

Of cases in which Judicial Rents have been Fixed by the Civil Bill Courts and notified to the Irish Land Commission during the month of October, 1885.

Province and County	Number of Holdings in which Rents have been fixed	Acreage	Tenement Valuation	Former Rent	Judicial Rent
		Statute Acres.	£ s. d.	£ s. d.	£ s. d.
ULSTER					
Cavan,	70	1,537 0 23½	878 13 0	1,091 3 1	873 1 1
Londonderry,	1	18 0 35	31 10 0	6 0 0	13 0 0
Monaghan,	1	37 1 30	30 0 0	28 4 0	19 4 0
Tyrone,	2	39 1 33	18 10 0	21 16 0	17 0 0
Total,	74	1,612 2 9½	329 13 0	1,148 0 1	879 5 1
LEINSTER					
Kildare,	1	61 0 39	42 0 0	50 7 1	70 0 0
Kilkenny,	6	230 1 35	113 15 0	156 9 11	199 13 6
Longford,	6	96 0 37	65 0 0	91 16 3	65 13 9
Westmeath,	1	16 1 13	10 10 0	11 2 0	13 10 0
Total,	14	109 0 34	252 3 0	312 15 11	277 16 3
CONNAUGHT					
Leitrim,	1	41 2 33	18 10 0	16 10 0	13 0 0
Mayo,	6	80 0 25	30 3 0	54 16 5	35 14 6
Roscommon,	7	39 1 13	5 15 0	11 3 1	7 1 6
Total,	9	143 1 1	51 13 0	81 13 0	55 16 2
MUNSTER					
Cork,	6	357 0 0	66 10 0	112 3 4	73 3 10
Kerry,	1	43 0 0	37 0 0	53 0 0	23 0 0
Limerick,	6	226 1 3	51 3 0	131 3 6	85 10 0
Waterford,	9	718 3 37	314 3 0	301 6 6	354 10 0
Total,	22	1,353 0 29	459 0 0	597 16 10	354 3 10

IRELAND.

	Number	Acreage	Tenement Valuation	Former Rent	Judicial Rent
ULSTER,	74	1,612 3 9½	329 13 0	1,148 0 1	879 5 1
LEINSTER,	14	409 0 14	252 3 0	312 15 11	277 16 3
CONNAUGHT,	9	143 1 1	51 13 0	81 13 0	55 16 2
MUNSTER,	22	1,353 0 29	459 0 0	602 16 10	354 3 10
Total,	119	3,517 0 2½	1,702 11 0	2,845 6 10	1,847 3 4

Grand Jury Cess Payers	No.	Name of Tenant	Name of Landlord	Townland
George Watson, q.c.	960	Edward Derry,	Lady Lisgar,	Corraghry,
	961	Michael Magee,	John Brady,	Drumbart,
	962	Patrick Brady,	Chas. O'Reilly, Committee of Owen McMahon, a lunatic,	Tarmylin,
	963	Francis McKiernan,	Emily J. Lloyd and others,	Coolnacra,
	964	Patrick McGovern, assr.	Caroline Hutton,	Cortecann,
	965	Edward Reilly,	do.	Mohera,
	966	Owen McGovern,	do.	do.
	967	Farrell Reilly,	do.	Maherinch,
	968	Ellen Dermott,	do.	Mahera,
	969	Peter Heary,	do.	do.
	970	Thomas Murphy,	do.	do.
	971	Francis Heary,	do.	do.
	972	Robert Thompson,	do.	Oalka,
	973	John Murray,	do.	Mahera,
	974	John Fitzpatrick,	Henry Dobbing,	Arnaghre,
	975	Edward Fitzpatrick,	Patrick Sheridan and assr.	Legwval,
	976	Hugh McCabe,	Henry Dobbing,	Arnaghm,
	977	Patrick McMahon,	J. D. Rushford,	Derrycranny,
	978	George Beary,	Earl of Gosford,	Gartelough,
	979	David Campbellow,	do.	Cardowran,
	980	Robert Elliott,	do.	Gartelough,
	981	William Elliott,	do.	do.
	982	Alexander Wilson,	do.	Branklill,
	983	Thomas Grumes,	George McCabe,	Larraghvearra,
	984	Hugh Reilly,	Hon. Clara Annesley,	Arnaklin,
	985	Michael Corry,	do.	Aughnarskita,
	986	Rose A. McKiernan,	do.	do.
	987	John Latimer,	do.	do.
	988	James Hanagan,	Chas. O'Reilly, Committee of Owen McMahon, a lunatic	Tarmylin,
	989	Patrick Coll,	Neil Annesley,	Drumbove,

ULSTER.

CAVAN.

Extent of Holdings. Statute	Poor Law Valuation.	Former Rent.	Judicial R.	Observations.	Tithe of Tenancy.
A. R. P.	£ s. d.	£ s. d.	£ s. d.		£ s.
5 3 17	5 0 0	5 5 5	5 0 0		
0 3 33	7 0 0	5 5 0	1 0 0		
18 1 18	15 5 0	17 5 5	15 16 0		
23 3 35	9 15 0	11 0 0	9 13 6		
19 0 36	8 15 0	11 7 0	9 5 0		
13 0 11	5 10 0	5 15 0	3 15 0		
17 2 5	5 15 0	10 10 0	8 10 0		
10 5 37	6 10 0	7 15 5	5 15 0		
30 5 53	15 5 0	17 18 0	14 10 0		
15 5 21	8 0 0	9 1 5	7 10 0		
18 2 31	9 0 0	10 11 0	5 16 0		
25 2 15	10 0 0	15 5 5	10 0 0		
51 3 13	11 7 0	15 15 5	11 5 0		
30 1 59	8 10 0	5 10 0	7 0 0		
16 1 17	5 0 0	5 0 0	5 0 0		
9 3 33	5 5 0	5 0 0	3 15 0		
15 0 31	7 10 0	18 0 0	1 3 5		
27 5 18	7 11 0	8 5 5	7 0 0		
20 1 33	15 10 0	13 18 10	11 0 0		
11 2 53	5 10 0	5 15 5	5 0 5		
5 3 11	5 3 0	5 15 3	5 10 0		
17 0 1	15 0 0	18 7 5	11 9 0		
15 3 1	8 15 0	10 7 9	5 15 0		
5 1 19	8 5 0	5 5 5	3 5 0		
31 0 31	20 5 5	29 5 5	20 0 0		
5 0 55	not valued,	5 0 0	3 10 0		
15 3 15	31 0 0	15 0 0	21 0 0		
9 2 1	5 15 0	9 0 0	5 2 5		
5 0 10	2 10 0	5 5 5	5 15 0		
11 1 9	5 15 0	11 0 0	7 5 0		

County Court Judge	No	Name of Tenant	Name of Landlord	Townland
George Waters, q.c.	990	Thomas Connolly,	Earl Annesley,	Milltown,
	991	Edward Cannan,	do	Drumburn,
	992	Philip Gilderman,	do	Milltown,
	993	Do	do	Drumgrah,
	994	Owen Cahill,	do	Tonnymmully,
	995	Thomas Kelly,	Charles Williams,	Aughnabran,
	996	William Colvell,	Benjamin S. Adams,	Dromard,
	997	Terence Brady,	do	do
	998	John Reilly,	Thomas Gerrard,	Clennalen,
	999	Hugh McGurgan,	do	do
	1000	Patrick McCaffrey,	do	do
	1001	John Brady,	do	do
	1002	John Maguire,	Marcus Davis and another,	Failtren,
	1003	John Connell,	John Burns,	Drumnargan,
	1004	Alexander McConnell,	John M. Holton and another,	Barren,
	1005	Catherine Mulaney,	do	do
	1006	Patrick Juggan,	do	Coolraghan
	1007	Francis Bannon,	do	do
	1008	Patrick Mulaney,	do	Barren,
	1009	Peter Smith,	do	Coolraghan,
	1010	John Flynn,	do	Barren,
	1011	James Bannon,	do	Coolraghan,
	1012	Elizabeth Mulaney,	do	Barren,
	1013	Michael Montague,	do	Coolraghan,
	1014	William Jackson,	Lord Farnham,	Remah,
	1015	Catherine Johnston,	John W. Standard,	Edgarton,
	1016	Peter Wright,	Frederick F. O'Carroll,	Crisha,
	1017	John Reilly,	do	do
	1018	Farrell Reilly,	do	do
	1019	Charles Lynch,	do	do
	1020	Thomas Reilly,	John Leslie,	Curraragh, Upper,
	1021	Bernard Brady,	Trustees of Devisees of Castlethorn,	Drumkurren,
	1022	Bernard Corrigan,	do	do
	1023	Philip Fitzpatrick,	do	do
	1024	John Reilly,	do	Tanagh

Extent of Holding in acres	Poor Law Valuation.	Present Rent.	Judicial Rent.	Observations	Value of Tenantry.
a. r. p.	£ s. d.	£ s. d.	£ s. d.		£ s. d.
22 3 10	13 0 0	24 0 0	18 8 0		
30 2 11	21 5 0	28 5 0	20 0 0		
4 3 3	8 5 0	7 8 0	4 15 0		
15 2 3	10 0 0	13 10 0	11 0 0		
15 1 21	10 5 0	10 11 1	9 10 0		
1 2 9½	4 10 0	4 15 0	4 0 0		
208 0 0	155 0 0	174 8 4	150 0 0		
9 1 22	8 0 0	10 0 0	8 14 0		
16 0 24	14 8 0	14 12 5	13 5 0		
4 2 17	4 1 0	4 7 4	3 12 0		
16 3 4	12 0 0	15 0 0	12 10 0		
19 2 34	14 10 0	16 16 0	13 0 0		
4 0 0	2 11 0	4 0 0	3 0 0		
1 2 8	1 10 0	5 10 0	3 0 0		
17 3 10	6 16 0	9 11 0	7 0 0		
22 1 22	17 10 0	22 7 8	15 17 0		
65 3 31	33 0 0	36 14 0	32 0 0		
10 1 21	8 5 0	8 11 0	7 10 0		
16 2 19	6 0 0	11 6 5	7 14 0		
11 3 11	7 0 0	10 16 8	7 0 0		
40 0 2	17 15 0	20 18 2	16 12 0		
10 0 20	4 15 0	6 0 0	4 0 0		
9 2 15	5 0 0	5 8 0	4 0 0		
16 2 25	8 0 0	11 10 4	8 3 0		
31 1 20	18 15 0	34 0 0	20 0 0		
80 0 2	55 15 0	70 0 0	60 0 0		
23 2 26	18 15 0	21 5 4	11 0 0		
9 2 15	4 5 0	10 3 4	6 10 0		
20 2 16	13 10 0	18 0 0	14 0 0		
16 0 8	10 5 0	16 11 5	12 10 0		
10 1 2	4 15 0	6 0 0	4 10 0		
16 2 19	9 8 0	13 4 0	9 0 0		
21 1 24	17 5 0	22 15 0	18 0 0		
13 1 31	4 5 0	6 12 0	7 0 0		
37 1 27	12 15 0	15 0 0	13 15 0		

County Court Judge	No.	Name of Tenant	Name of Landlord	Townland
Lambert Watkins, q.c.	1025	Thomas	Trustees of Countess of Castle	Toningh, —
	1026	Do., ...	do.	Drumkeerun, —
	1047	Henry .... —	Lord Farnham, ... —	Curragow, —
	1028	Do.,	do, ...	Drumtom, ..
	1029	William Upham, ...	do	Zessuk, ..
				Total, —

J. C. Kullar, q.c.	1	Samuel Doyle,	Alice O'Neill and others, ..	Cough,

W. N. Barton,	113	Alexander Hall,	Margaret Faworth,	Cloghrough, ...

Rev. F. W. Brand	376	Ellen Quinn,	Nathaniel Mayne,	Turbotson, —
	373	Robert McMullan,	Jonathan Clarke,	Tallybern, —
				Total, —

29 7 3½	29 13 6	26 6 8	22 0 0
1,377 7 3¾	579 13 0	1,094 3 1	878 1 1

LONDONDERRY.

14 0 3½	31 10 0	6 0 0	15 0 0

PROVINCE OF

COUNTY OF

County Court Judge.	No.	Name of Tenant.	Name of Landlord.	Townland.
W. F. Darley, q.c.	4	Patrick Gavin,	Thomas Hendrick,	Tally,

COUNTY OF

T. ... Mohern, q c	39	James Brennan,	Thomas Traison,	M'Birney,
	40	Thomas Keeffe,	do.	do.
	41	Michael Dowling,	Miss Dorothea Bexley,	Barrinnmn,
	42	Do.	do.	do.
	43	Anastatia Ryan.	Mrs. Dora Morgan,	Gasltown,
	44	Michael Holden,	Reps. of David Webb,	Llannatrego,
				Total,

COUNTY OF

John Arye Cranan, q c	251	Hugh Cregan,	Earl of Grannard,	Menuluff,
	252	John Healy,	George W. Gunning,	Fubernstown,
	253	Anna Gunney,	Archdeacon Henry Stewart,	Dunogue,
	254	Mary Keegan, Rep. of John Keegan,	Charles Atkinson,	Furgney,
	255	John Trimble,	Chas. R. James and another, Assignees of Thos. C. Breslan,	Drumluh,
	256	Rose O'Reilly,	Andrew Brook,	Gurtrenter & esar.
				Total,

COUNTY OF

LEINSTER

KILDARE.

Extent of Holding. Acres.	Poor Law Valuation.	Former Rent.	Judicial Rent.	Observations.	Value of Tenancy.
a. r. p.	£ s. d.	£ s. d.	£ s. d.		£ s. d.
64 0 27	65 0 0	50 7 1	70 0 0		

KILKENNY.

35 0 31	13 0 0	23 5 1	17 0 0	
1 0 0	not valued.	1 0 0	0 10 0	
5 3 22	2 10 0	4 3 6	4 8 6	
94 1 12	33 5 6	19 0 5	60 0 0	
16 1 30	29 0 0	5 0 0	33 0 0	
11 2 16	29 0 0	38 4 1	38 0 0	
150 1 35	113 15 0	136 9 11	156 13 6	

LONGFORD.

3 2 0	4 10 0	3 5 0	1 5 0
25 0 31	18 5 0	25 0 0	18 10 0
14 0 31	9 15 0	9 0 0	8 10 0
1 3 21	1 0 0	9 0 0	5 17 0
10 0 11	8 10 0	9 0 0	7 15 0
30 0 53	30 0 0	34 4 8	25 0 0
85 0 27	65 0 0	92 14 8	66 13 0

WESTMEATH.

18 1 14	19 10 0	14 2 0	19 10 0

County Court Judge	No.	Name of Tenant	Name of Landlord	Townland
George Watson, Q C	667	James Robb, senior, ...	William Johnston, ...	Fingrough, Upper.

J B Bayward	2469	Hugh Murtagh, ...	G. A. Moore, ...	Art, ...
	2470	Thomas McLoughlin, .	do.	do. ...
	2471	Thomas Campbell, ...	Letitia A. M. McDonnell and another,	Johnsfort, ...
	2472	Anthony McDonagh, ...	Anthony G. Carey, ...	Shanaghy, ...
	2473	Patt Brown, ...	Edmund R. Perry, ...	Knockmore, ...
	2474	Michael Kenny, ..	Miss Knox, ...	Tullyquin, ...
				Total, ...

CONNAUGHT.

LEITRIM.

Extent of Holding, Statute.	Poor Law Valuation	Tenant Rent	Judicial Rent	Observations	Value Tenancy.
A. R. P.	£ s. d	£ s. d	£ s. d		£ s. d
41 2 17	18 10 0	15 10 0	15 0 0		

MAYO.

15 3 19	6 10 0	11 0 0	7 10 6		
13 0 2	5 6 0	8 9 2	9 16 0		
11 1 30	5 0 0	9 15 0	5 10 0		
16 3 0	6 0 0	13 1 6	8 0 0		
18 1 10	7 15 0	10 0 0	8 0 0		
6 0 0	5 13 0	4 13 0	4 0 0		
80 0 35	33 8 0	51 18 8	35 16 6		

ROSCOMMON.

Crary Court Judge.	No.	Name of Tenant.	Name of Landlord.	Townland.
Robert Ferguson, q.c.	133	George W French, ...	John H. Hunter, ...	East Gully, ...
	234	Michael Tuohig, ...	Allan J. Lee, ...	Lahinch-road, ...
	135	Bartholomew Hourihan,	Adam Newman, ...	Hillsanbrnes, ...
	238	Cornelius Sullivan, ...	James L. Notter, ...	Boulinlagh, ...
				Total, ...

W. O'C. Morris,	99	Morty Barkley, ...	Reps. of George Chute, ...	Shroac, ...

T. A. Purcell, q.c.	194	John O'Grady, ...	John W. Seymour, ...	Monshraher, ...
	195	Edmund Sheehan, ...	Anne B. Chaddeld, ...	Tubbernurry, ...
	196	Richard M. Woulfe, ...	Trustees of Archdeacon Gould,	Craddes, West, ...
	197	James Cuthbert, ...	Trustees of Lyons, & others, ...	Cappaimaig, ...
	198	Daniel Nolan, ...	Assignees of Wm. A. Guggie and another,	Scart, ...
	199	David Connolly, ...	do.	Glenagragra, ...
	200	Patrick Mulqueen, ...	Maryute Della Locello and another,	Knockboylene, ...
	201	John Enright, ...	do.	Dunrahin, ...
				Total, ...

George Waters, q.c.	100	Margaret Morrison, ...	Lady B. White, ...	Knockane, South, ...
	168	Do., ...	do.	Knockane, North, ...
	110	Bridget Cahill, ...	W. B. Jackson, ...	Farano, ...

MUNSTER.

CORK.

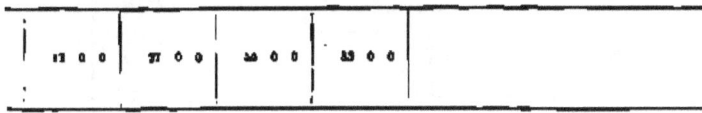

Extent of Holding, Statute.	Poor Law Valuation.	Former Rent.	Judicial Rent.	Observations.	Value of Tenancy.
A. R. P.	£ s. d.	£ s. d.	£ s. d.		£ s. d.
17 3 24	34 15 0	67 0 0	37 5 6		
807 0 0	20 15 0	15 0 0	80 0 0		
18 0 0	7 10 0	5 0 0	7 8 4		
19 1 16	1 10 0	5 5 0	3 10 0		
881 0 0	64 10 0	112 5 0	76 3 10		

KERRY.

12 0 0	27 0 0	44 0 0	83 0 0		

LIMERICK.

COUNTY OF WATERFORD (continued)

County Court Judge	No.	Name of Tenant	Name of Landlord	Townland	Former Fair Rent Rent	Poor Law Valuation	Former Rent	Judicial Rent	Observations	Value of Tenancy
Queens Waterford, &c.	191	Daniel Hearn	Most Rev. Dr. Power	Ardmore						
	192	Thomas More	Thomas Fleming	Ballynacourty						
	193	Lawrence Fitzgerald	John Welsh	Ballylemon						
	194	John Lynch	do.	do.						
	195	William Jordan	Makomara, executors	Ballynamuck						
	196	David Keane	John O'Brady and another	Ballinamona						
				Total, —						

Rents fixed upon the Reports of Valuers appointed by the Irish Land Commission on the joint applications of Landlords and Tenants.

No.	Place of Issue	Name of Landlord	Townland	Poor Law Valuation	Former Rent	Judicial Rent